George Brown, CLASS CLOWN

World's Worst Wedgie

by Nancy Krulik
illustrated by Aaron Blecha

SCHOLASTIC INC.
New York Toronto London Auckland
Sydney Mexico City New Delhi Hong Kong

For Danny, who loves to laugh.–NK

For Joel–brother, best friend and favorite
wedgie victim.–AB

ISBN 978-0-545-33278-1

Text copyright © 2010 by Nancy Krulik.
Illustrations copyright © 2010 by Aaron Blecha.
All rights reserved. Published by Scholastic Inc.,
557 Broadway, New York, NY 10012, by arrangement with
Grosset & Dunlap, a division of Penguin Young Readers Group,
a member of Penguin Group (USA) Inc. SCHOLASTIC and associated
logos are trademarks and/or registered trademarks of Scholastic Inc.

12 11 10 9 8 7 6 5 4 3 2 1   11 12 13 14 15 16/0

Printed in the U.S.A.   40

First Scholastic printing, January 2011

Chapter 1

"Check this out, you guys!"

George Brown took off down the block on his skateboard. It popped up and spun around in midair before George landed on it and rolled down the street.

George smiled. **Now *that* was some serious liftoff!**

"Whoa!" George's friend Alex cheered. "When did you learn that?"

"Yesterday," George said. "At Tyler's Toy Shop."

"They give skateboarding lessons there?" George's other friend Chris asked.

"No," George said. "But they had this really cool remote-controlled toy called **Dude-on-a-Skateboard**. I played with it and this was one of the tricks you could make it do. Then I practiced doing it myself later."

"So will your parents buy it for you?" Chris asked.

George shook his head. "Forget it. It was

fifteen dollars. They said if I want it so
badly, I can save up my allowance."

Alex shrugged. "I guess you're not
getting it anytime
soon."

"What's that
supposed to mean?"
George asked.

"Nothing," Alex said.
"It's just that you're
lousy at saving money."

"Yeah," Chris agreed. "Remember that
time you went to the comic book store
with me? You bought three comics, ones
you don't even like."

"Or the last time we
went to the penny candy
store?" Alex asked.

"You blew three dollars
there. No one can eat
three hundred pieces

of penny candy. But you had three bucks, so you spent three bucks."

George didn't answer Chris or Alex. What could he say? They were right. George *was* a lousy saver.

George rode the rest of the way to school on his skateboard while Chris and Alex walked behind him. When they reached the school yard, they saw a big crowd of fourth-graders gathered by one of the big oak trees.

"What's going on?" Chris asked.

George skateboarded over to find out.

Louie was standing in the middle of the group—with a remote control in his hands. George looked down and watched the Dude-on-a-Skateboard spin around in a perfect 360. **How come Louie was always the first one to get anything cool?**

"Check it out!" Louie told the kids. "I can make my RC Dude-on-a-Skateboard **pop a wheelie!**"

"Pretty cool!" Julianna said.

"Can I try?" George asked.

"Why should I let you?" Louie asked.

"Umm, because it's nice to share?" George suggested.

"I *am* sharing," Louie told him.

"*How* are you sharing?" George asked.

"I'm letting you watch," Louie told him.

"See?" Max said, turning to George. "He told you he was sharing."

George frowned. He started to say how sharing had a whole different meaning in Louie's world. But he stopped mid-sentence and shut his mouth tight.

Louie didn't seem to notice. He was too busy flicking the switch on his remote. All the kids were watching the Dude-on-a-Skateboard whirl around in circles.

All except George. He couldn't watch. He was too freaked out by the bubbles that had suddenly started bouncing around in his belly. **There was a burp brewing in there.** And not just any burp. From the way those bubbles were bing-bonging around, George could tell this was a *super burp*. **It wanted out**, but there was no way George was going to let *that* happen!

All of a sudden, he began to spin around and around in circles. He wanted to force

that burp to swirl its way back down to his toes—just the way water swirls its way back down the toilet after you flush.

"Yo! Check out George!" Alex said. The kids all turned to watch George spin around and around in circles.

"Hey!" Louie shouted. "Are you making fun of my Dude-on-a-Skateboard?"

George wasn't making fun of anything. He was just trying to **squelch a belch**. But he couldn't tell Louie that. The super burp was George's secret. And he was going to keep it that way.

Chapter 2

It had all started on George's first day at Edith B. Sugarman Elementary School. George's family had moved—again. That meant George was the new kid—again. George's dad was in the army, so his family moved around a lot.

This time, George had promised himself that he was **turning over a new leaf**. No more pranks. No more class clown. He wasn't going to get into any trouble anymore, like he had at all his old schools.

At first, it really worked. George raised his hand before answering questions. He didn't make faces or laugh behind teachers' backs.

But George didn't have to be a math whiz like his pal Alex to figure out how many friends being a new, well-behaved kid would get him. The answer was easy. **Zero. Nada. Zilch.**

That night, George's parents took him out to Ernie's Ice Cream Emporium. While they were sitting outside and George was finishing his root beer float, a shooting star flashed across the sky. So George made a wish.

I want to make kids laugh—but not get into trouble.

Unfortunately, the star was gone before George could finish the wish. So only half came true—**the first half**.

A minute later, George had a funny feeling in his belly. It was like there were hundreds of tiny bubbles bouncing around in there. The bubbles ping-ponged their way into his chest and bing-bonged their way up into his throat. And then . . .

George let out a big burp. A *huge* burp. A SUPER burp!

The super burp was loud, and it was *magical*.

Suddenly George lost control of his arms and legs. It was like they had minds of their own. His hands grabbed straws and stuck them up his nose like a walrus. His feet jumped up on the table and started dancing. **Everyone at Ernie's started laughing**— except George's parents, who were covered in ice cream from the sundaes he had knocked over.

That wasn't the only time the super burp had burst its way out of George's belly. George never knew when a burp would strike or what it would make him do. Like juggle raw eggs in his classroom (which would have been fine if George actually knew *how* to

juggle) or make his
model volcano erupt
in red goo all over his
teacher or dive-bomb
the audience during
a talent show.

Every time the
burp came, George
made the other kids
laugh. But he also
managed to make grown-ups **really mad**.

That was why George was
determined to keep this burp
from bursting out. He didn't
know what he might do if
it exploded out of him.
But he did know where
he would wind up:
in trouble. *And* in the
principal's office.

So George kept spinning

15

and spinning, trying to force that burp down the drain.

Whoosh. Suddenly George felt a huge bubble pop inside his stomach. All the air rushed right out of him. The fizzy feeling was gone.

All right! **George had beaten the burp!** He stopped spinning and pumped his fist in the air.

"What was that all about?" Louie asked.

George had to say something—fast!

"It's your fault," George told Louie. "You were making me spin."

"Huh?" Louie asked.

"It's that remote control," George said. "It's sending signals to the metal filling in my tooth. It's making me spin, see?"

The kids all started laughing.

"Hey, it's making me spin, too," Chris added. He began whirling around and around.

A minute later all the kids were spinning in circles. Well, **almost** all of them, anyway. Max and Mike stopped spinning after Louie shot them dirty looks.

"You are **so weird**," Louie told George.

George shrugged. He didn't mind Louie calling him weird. It was better than Louie calling him crazy. And crazy was definitely what Louie would think if George ever told him about the super burp.

Chapter 3

"George, can you tell us the name of the capital of Alaska?"

Uh-oh. Mrs. Kelly had caught him doodling in his notebook. The old George hardly ever paid attention in class. But **the new George didn't daydream**. At least not too often.

"Um . . . I . . . ," George mumbled.

A few of the kids started to giggle.

Mrs. Kelly gave George a gummy smile. George wasn't used to having teachers like him, but for some reason, Mrs. Kelly did. "It's okay," she said. "We all have days when we are a little foggy. And *you know* a lot about geography." Mrs. Kelly said the words "you know" really loud.

Huh? If he knew a lot, he would know the capital. **Wait a minute.** Maybe Mrs. Kelly was giving him a hint.

"*You know* Alaska's capital, George. I'm sure *you know* it."

George tried to figure out what Mrs. Kelly was telling him. Then it hit him. **You know—*Juneau*!**

"The capital of Alaska is Juneau," George shouted out.

Mrs. Kelly nodded and gave George another gummy smile. "Exactly. Juneau, Alaska."

"Class, let me show you some pictures of my trip to Alaska," Mrs. Kelly said as she clicked the mouse on her computer. A picture of Mrs. Kelly in front of a totem pole appeared on the screen in the front of the room. "Here I am in a national park in Sitka, Alaska."

The face that was carved in the totem pole right above Mrs. Kelly's head had **big, buggy eyes** and a **funny, toothy frown**. It was exactly the upside down of Mrs. Kelly's big, toothy smile. George poked Alex, who sat next to him, and started to make the totem pole face. But then he stopped . . . that was *so* old George.

"And here I am on an iceberg," Mrs. Kelly said, changing the picture. "I had to fly there in a helicopter."

There was Mrs. Kelly, standing on a white block of ice.

Mrs. Kelly clicked the computer mouse again. Up came another picture of Mrs. Kelly on the iceberg. This time she was lying on the ice, with one leg in front of her, and one to the side. Her glasses were all crooked.

Mrs. Kelly quickly clicked the mouse. "Um . . . **the iceberg was really slippery**," she explained.

George made sure not to look at Alex.
If he did, he knew he'd burst out laughing.

"Here I am beating a real Alaskan drum,"
Mrs. Kelly said. "And for a special treat, I've
brought the drum in to show you."

Mrs. Kelly held up a big drum. The head
of the drum was the size of a **pizza**. A picture
of a red and blue bird with a big beak was
painted on it.

George sure hoped Mrs. Kelly wasn't going to do something weird like start banging on that drum or anything. If she did, it would be *impossible* for him not to laugh.

Before George could even finish his thought, Mrs. Kelly began banging the drum, and chanting some Native American song she'd learned from the Tlingit tribe in Alaska.

"Dei yin d'tawn," his teacher sang. "Xaan woo jee xee na."

The song was probably really cool when it was sung by someone who knew how it was supposed to go. **But Mrs. Kelly couldn't sing.** She couldn't drum very well, either.

BOOM BOOM BOOM

"Hee hee yaaa," Mrs. Kelly screeched at the top of her lungs. "Hee hee yaw aanna."

George picked up his pencil and started to draw another Dude-on-a-Skateboard in his notebook. **It was the only way to stop himself from laughing at Mrs. Kelly.**

George twirled his pencil and started thinking. He got two dollars a week for his allowance. If he saved every penny, in eight weeks, he'd have more than enough money for the Dude-on-a-Skateboard.

Suddenly, George realized something important. It had nothing to do with totem poles, icebergs, or drums, though. He didn't have to wait weeks and save up. George was going to make that money, and make it **fast**.

George Brown was a man with a plan!

Chapter 4

"Mom!" George shouted on his way into the Knit Wit.

George's mom's store was a really boring place. It was full of crafty stuff like yarn, cloth, glitter, and silk flowers.

There was usually a bunch of ladies sitting around with knitting needles saying stuff like "knit one . . . purl two." Every now and then, one of them would threaten to knit a hat with a pom-pom for George because he was "just so darn cute."

He was ready to put his plan into action! "Mom!" George yelled again.

George's mother came racing out of the stock room. "What's the matter?"

"Nothing," George said. "I just wanted to talk to you."

"So talk. I'm all ears," his mom said.

"Do you need any help around here?" George said.

George's mom gave him a curious look. "You want to help me . . . *here*?"

George understood why his mom sounded so surprised. "Yeah," he said. "I thought you could give me a job."

"Why do you need a job?" George's mom asked.

"Well, I want that remote-controlled skateboard, and you said I had to pay for it. So . . ." George let his voice trail off.

"I don't know, George," his mom said.

George cocked his head to the side, and flashed his mom **a goofy, crooked smile**.

"Oh no, not your special face," his mom said.

George smiled harder. Oh *yes*. His mom could never refuse George anything when he made his **special face**.

George's mom laughed. "All right. I guess it won't do any harm to have you straighten up the shelves. And I could use someone to sort the beads. The trays are a mess."

"I'm great at cleaning up messes," George said.

"Since when?" his mom teased.

"Since right now," George promised.

A few minutes later, George was busy in the back of the store straightening up. **It was a pretty boring job.** But George didn't complain. His mom was paying him five dollars an hour. That meant all he had to do was hang in there for three hours and that RC Dude-on-a-Skateboard would be **all his**.

COTTON THREAD YARN

Once George had everything stacked up, he headed toward the bead department. And that's when he felt the bubbles—*big* bubbles. And they were all bouncing around in his belly. **Uh-oh!** Those bubbles could only mean one thing. **The super burp!**

Oh man! Not again. Two times in one day! That just wasn't fair.

George held his nose and clamped his

mouth shut. Then he started jumping up and down, trying to force the bubbles down.

A little girl pointed to George. "Why is that boy acting so silly, Mommy?" she asked.

George had already kept one burp inside

today. But this one seemed determined to get out.

The bubbles ping-pong-pinged their way up out of George's stomach.

They boing-bing-boinged their way to his chest.

They bing-boing-binged their way up his throat. And then . . .

B·U·U·U·R·P!

George let out a humongous burp! **The kind of burp that could be heard all the way in Juneau, Alaska.**

"George!" his mother scolded.

George opened his mouth to say, "Excuse me." But that's not what came out. Instead, George let out a loud, angry, monsterlike sound. He didn't mean to.

But George wasn't in control. The super burp had taken over. His arms and legs were on their own. His hands grabbed a big roll of pink and purple, polka-dotted cloth. His body began to spin around and around, getting all wrapped up in the material.

George's arms stuck themselves straight out and his legs began walking stiffly around the store **like a mummy in a scary movie**.

"I want my mummy!" George's mouth shouted.

"George! Stop that this minute!" his mother shouted.

But George didn't stop. He couldn't. **The super burp was in charge now.**

"That boy is funny, Mommy," the little girl by the silk flowers said.

Her sister started laughing, too.

"George!" George's mom didn't think he was funny. Not one bit.

George's body turned itself around.

His hands found a big tray of beads. They tilted the tray and . . .

Ping! Ping! Ping! Hundreds of small black and silver beads fell all over the floor.

Whoops! George's feet slid over the beads.

Wham! George's rear end bashed onto the floor. *Ow!* That one hurt.

"Arrooo!" George shouted. He sounded like a mummy in pain.

Whoosh. Suddenly, George felt something go pop in his stomach like someone had punctured a balloon. All the air rushed out of him. The super burp was gone!

But George was still lying there on the floor. He wasn't a mummy anymore. He was just a kid, wrapped up in a pink and purple, polka-dotted cloth. And he was in **big trouble**.

"George, look at this mess!" his mother demanded. "What got into you?"

George didn't know what to say. The problem wasn't what had gotten *into* him. It was what had slipped **out** **of** **him**. But he couldn't tell his mother about the super burp. She wouldn't believe him. She'd just think he was making a crazy excuse for his behavior. So he just opened his mouth and said, "I'm sorry. I'll clean up everything."

"You bet you will," his mother told him. "And then you'll go straight home."

"Home?" George asked. "But what about my job?"

"You don't have a job anymore," his mom said.

George couldn't believe his ears. He'd just been **fired** by his own mother. That wasn't fair. It was the stupid super burp that deserved to be fired and sent packing—anywhere. To any other kid. Because **George Brown was *sick* of burping**.

Chapter 5

"How much have you saved up?" Chris asked the next morning before school.

George felt one lonely **quarter** in his pocket. "Not much, I passed an ice cream truck yesterday."

"You bought an ice cream with the allowance money you were supposed to be saving?" Alex shook his head.

George needed ice cream after leaving his mom's store but no way was he going

into the
whole
polka-dotted
mummy
thing. So he
just said, "It
was one of
those ice creams that
looked like a cat. It had red
bubble gum eyeballs."

"I love those," Chris said.

"Me too," Alex agreed.
"But that doesn't help George
get an RC toy."

They watched Louie in the school
yard. He'd brought **Dude** with him again.

"He's just showing off," George said.

"He's charging kids a nickel to play
with it," Alex said.

"Hey! What if we pooled our money?"
George suggested. "Then we could get an

RC Dude-on-a-Skateboard and share it. Really share it. **Not _Louie_-share it**."

"That would be awesome," Chris said. "Except for one thing."

"What's that?" George asked.

"I have exactly a nickel," Chris answered.

"I only have eleven cents," Alex said. "But I borrowed a dollar from my mom last week. So that means counting all three of us, **we really have minus fifty-nine cents**."

It was pretty impressive how Alex could do math problems in his head. But having minus fifty-nine cents was **definitely not**.

"Maybe we could earn the money selling stuff," Chris suggested.

"Like what?" Alex asked. "Your comic books?"

"No way!" Chris said. "What about a lemonade stand?"

"So many kids have lemonade stands," Alex said.

"Listen," George told his friends, "my mom is always making gourmet stuff from cookbooks. Gourmet means it's better than plain old food. We're not going to sell ordinary lemonade at our stand . . . we're going to sell **gourmet lemonade!**"

"I'm worried because we didn't put in enough sugar," Alex told George. It was Saturday afternoon. The boys were lugging all the stuff for their lemonade stand to the playground.

"We used up all the sugar my mom had," George reminded him. "Anyway, remember, this is gourmet lemonade. It's not **supposed** to taste like plain old lemonade."

"I put in extra lemon juice to make up for the missing sugar," Chris said.

"Exactly," George said. "The more lemons the better. It's called lemonade. Not **sugarade**."

Alex found a shady spot beneath a tree, and Chris helped him open up the card table they'd borrowed from Alex's house.

George taped their sign to the table. It said: **"Gourmet" Lemonade! Only 10c A Cup!** Then he put the pitcher of lemonade and a stack of paper cups on the table.

"We're only charging **ten cents a cup**?" Alex said. "Do you guys know how long it will take us to earn fifteen dollars?"

"Kids don't have a lot of money," George told Alex. "We can't charge more."

"That's true," Alex admitted.

"Now let's get us some customers,"

George said. He reached into his
backpack and pulled out a long, yellow
sweatshirt and a yellow baseball hat
with long plastic straws coming out of
it. "One of you guys put these on."
Alex and Chris stared at him.

"GOURMET"
LEMONADE!
ONLY 10¢ A CUP!

"What?" they asked at the exact same time.

"This is how we advertise our gourmet lemonade," George explained.

"By putting on a hat?" Chris asked.

"It's not a hat," George told him. "It's part of **a lemonade costume**. One of you is going to dress up like a glass of lemonade and dance around."

"Why don't *you* wear it?" Alex suggested.

"Fine," George huffed. "I'll be the glass of lemonade." He slipped on the sweatshirt and the big, lemon yellow baseball hat with the giant straws hanging out of it. Then he began to **dance and sing**.

"When you're hot and really thirsty, lemonade's what you think of firsty . . ."

"Okay!" Alex shouted. "Get your gourmet lemonade! Cold, fresh lemonade!"

A few minutes later, Julianna and Sage rode by on their bikes.

Julianna looked at George and laughed. "Are you supposed to be a banana?"

"No," George said. "It's a lemonade costume to advertise our lemonade stand. **Why would I be dressed as a banana**?"

"I think you make a cute lemon, Georgie," Sage said.

George ignored Sage. He didn't like her calling him **cute**.

"We're trying to raise money to buy an RC Dude-on-a-Skateboard," Chris told the girls.

"We would let you play with ours for free," George said. "Want to buy some lemonade and help us out?"

"Okay." Julianna pulled a dime out of her pocket.

"Me too," Sage said. "I want to help you get your Dude, Georgie."

George poured the lemonade. **A customer was a customer.** Even if that customer was Sage.

"Whoa!" Julianna exclaimed after her first sip. "This is **sour**."

"It's *lemon*ade," Chris said. "Lemons are sour."

Sage took a sip. She made a face. "Wow. It's definitely lemony," she said.

Then she forced a smile and looked at
George. "But in a good way," she added.

"Didn't you put any sugar in?" Julianna
asked him.

"Some," Chris said. "But we didn't . . ."

George nudged Chris in the ribs. "We
didn't want to overpower the natural taste
of the lemons," George said. "This is a
gourmet citrus beverage."

Just then Louie, Max, and Mike showed up. Louie was holding a big, rubber ball.

"Bet you guys were playing killer ball." George said.

Louie nodded. Killer ball was a game Louie had made up. It was sort of like dodgeball, but **meaner**.

"You look like you need some lemonade," Alex told Mike and Max. "Playing killer ball can really make you thirsty."

Mike nodded. "And **black and blue**," he said.

Then he looked at Louie. "Not that I'm complaining," he added. "That's part of the game."

"What? Are you **a banana or something**?" Louie looked at George.

"No. I'm a lem—Oh, never mind," George said.

"This is gourmet lemonade," Sage told Louie.

"Yeah?" Louie asked. He plunked two dimes on the table. "Well, if it's that good, better make mine a double."

"GOURMET"
LEMONADE!

"Okay!" George said. He poured four glasses all the way to the top of the cup.

Max took a long sip of his lemonade. His lips pursed and he sucked in his cheeks. "Whoa!"

Mike tried his. He shut his eyes tight and shivered. **It looked like he had just swallowed medicine.** "It doesn't have enough sugar," he said.

Louie looked down at his cup. "I want my money back," he said.

Just then, three more kids came by.

They looked thirsty. So George ignored Louie and smiled.

But before George could say "Get your gourmet lemonade," a funny, bubbly feeling started up in his belly.

Oh no! The burp was back!

George wanted to beat the burp. He shut his mouth tight and pinched his nose.

"What are you doing?" Louie asked him.

George didn't answer. He *couldn't* answer. If he did, the burp would escape.

But this burp wasn't going to be kept down. It **bing-bonged** its way out of George's stomach and into his chest. Then it **ping-ponged** its way up into his throat. And then . . .

BUUURP!

George let out a **superduper megahumongous** burp! A burp so strong, it knocked the yellow baseball cap right off his head.

"Whoa!" Chris shouted. "That was major."

George's hands grabbed the glass out of Max's hands and poured the super-sour lemonade down George's throat.

Suddenly George's eyes got big and buggy. Then his hands reached up and grabbed his neck.

"Aahhh . . . I've been **poisoned!**" George shouted.

His feet began stumbling all around. His eyes crossed themselves.

"Cut it out! You're going to ruin our lemonade business," Alex said.

George knew that. And he wanted to stop but unfortunately, his body had a mind of its own. And it wanted to goof around some more.

"Gak . . . ," George said. His tongue popped out. "Good-bye, cruel world." He **plopped** down on the ground, and **wiggled** all around like a crazed snake.

Max and Mike started laughing. At least they did until Louie shot them a look.

And then . . .

Whoosh. George felt something pop in his belly. It was like the air had just rushed out of him. The super burp was **gone**!

"This kid's funny," one of the boys said.

"Yeah," his friend agreed. "But I'm not touching that lemonade."

"I'm out of here," the third kid agreed.

Louie, Max, and Mike weren't far behind. Pretty soon it was just George, Alex, Chris, Sage, and Julianna at the lemonade stand.

"George, are you sure you want to buy that Dude-on-a-Skateboard?" Alex asked him.

"Because it sure seems like you were trying to wreck the whole thing," Chris added. He sounded kind of **mad**.

George hadn't tried to wreck anything. The super burp had done that. But he knew there was no way he could tell his friends that. So he just mumbled, "I'm sorry."

Stupid super burp. **Now the whole plan had gone sour.**

Chapter 6

Monday morning in the school yard, Julianna came running over to George. She was bouncing a basketball in front of her as she ran.

"Think fast!" Julianna shouted. She threw the ball at George.

Oomph. The ball hit George right in the belly. He opened his mouth slightly, and . . . belch. A burp came flying out. **Not a big burp**. But a burp just the same.

George stood there for a minute. He waited for the magic to take over. But it didn't. *Phew.* That hadn't been a super burp. It was just a **nice, normal** burp.

"Hey, that reminds me," George said. "Did you guys ever hear the joke about the burp?"

"No," Alex said.

"Never mind," George said. "It's not worth repeating." He smiled. That had been a pretty funny joke. The kind of joke **a regular kid** would tell. Not a super burp kind of joke.

"You crack me up, George," Chris said.

Alex nodded. "Too bad you can't make money **clowning around**."

George stopped for a minute and stared at his pal. "Alex! You're a genius!" he shouted.

"I know how we can make a pile of money!" George paused. "It'll mean a lot of work."

"If I help you, can I share the Dude-on-a-Skateboard with you?" Julianna asked.

"Sure," George promised her.

"You'll be a **twenty-five percent owner**," Alex said.

"Okay. I'm in," Julianna said.

"So what's the plan?" Chris asked.

Out of the corner of his eye, George spotted Louie coming up the block to school with Mike and Max. The last thing George wanted was for Louie to hear his new plan. He'd find some way to ruin it.

"I'll tell you guys later," he said. "But I promise you're going to love this idea. It's my very best one yet!"

Chapter 7

By Saturday morning, George was completely convinced that his idea—a fabulous **one-ring backyard circus**—was his greatest money-making plan ever. Right then lots of little kids were arriving at Chris's backyard with their parents. And every one of them had bought a ticket!

The boys and Julianna had worked hard all week selling tickets and rehearsing their acts. George couldn't wait to perform his clown act for the kids. He was going to ride around on a tricycle and tell a bunch of jokes.

"I look like an idiot," Alex groaned as he stood in the middle of the garage putting on his costume. "This is **way too small**."

"That's because it's my sister's

Halloween costume from two years ago," Chris explained.

"Don't worry," George told Alex. "Chris looks like an idiot, too."

Chris was wearing **a tiger costume** that had a headband with ears. He looked in the mirror nailed to a wall and started painting whiskers on his face. "It was the only other animal costume we had."

"Quit complaining. We've already sold twenty tickets," George told his friends. "And I bet we sell lots of refreshments."

George could see Sage setting up the refreshment stand. They'd only let Sage help because she promised to bake a lot of cookies for free. Chris's mom had baked a **Boston cream pie**. The bottom of the pie was chocolate goo and on top of that was a mountain of whipped cream. It looked so good, George thought he'd buy a slice for himself after the show.

"Okay, okay." Alex sucked in his stomach really hard and pulled on the zipper until it closed. "I just want to know why Chris gets to be a tiger and I have to be a pig. When do you ever see a pig at a circus?"

"I told you before, you're not a pig. You're a **wild boar**," George told Alex. "Wild boars are fierce! Anyway, by noon, we'll be rich."

"We all look like idiots," Alex insisted.

George looked down at his clown costume. He was wearing a red wig, his mom's polka-dot shirt, and his dad's plaid golf pants. His red clown nose itched, and his dad's sneakers were like a **trillion** sizes too big.

Just then, Julianna arrived. She was wearing a top hat, a red shirt, and black pants tucked into horseback riding boots. She really did look like **a wild animal trainer**.

Julianna stared at Alex strangely. "You're a pig? I thought you were going to be a lion. Pigs aren't circus animals."

"We couldn't find the lion costume," Chris explained.

"And he's not a pig. He's a wild boar," George told her.

George took a peek outside and

smiled. Two rows of chairs were arranged in a big circle in the backyard and every seat was filled. It was a **sold-out show**!

"Looks like it's showtime!" George said.

George stepped into the middle of the circle—the center ring. "Ladies and gentlemen. Boys and girls," he shouted in his best circus voice. "Welcome to the Big Top. We have a great show for you today. First up: wild animal trainer Julianna and her ferocious beasts!"

Julianna ran into the center ring. Chris and Alex crawled behind her on all fours.

"Oh, Georgie," someone said suddenly. "Hi there."

George turned and saw Sage. She was wearing a bright green tutu and some green feathers in her hair. Sage was going to perform tricks on the trampoline in the backyard.

George hated it when Sage called him Georgie. The way she said it made it sound like she liked him or something. **George definitely didn't like being liked by Sage.**

"You're supposed to be at the refreshment stand," George said.

She smiled. "You look cute in that costume."

"I'm not supposed to be **cute**," George

said. "I'm supposed to be **funny**."

"Oh, you're funny, too, Georgie," she said.

"Don't call me Georgie!" he shouted.

"Oh, sorry," Sage said. "I mean you're very funny, *George*."

That was better.

"I've been practicing my twist on the trampoline. Is my acrobat act before or after your clown act?" Sage asked.

George didn't answer. Instead he kept his eyes on the center ring where Julianna was busy taming her animals. Chris the tiger had jumped through a hoop. Then he pretended to go wild, running around seats and roaring. Some of the little kids shrieked, but you could tell they knew it was only pretend.

"Now, ladies and gentlemen, the ferocious wild boar will do a somersault," Julianna said.

Alex crouched and tucked his head
down. But before he could roll over, there
was **a loud, ripping sound**. *R-r-r-ippp*.
Alex's costume tore right down the back.

The kids and their parents began
to laugh. George began to laugh, too.

And then, suddenly, he felt something bubbling **wildly** in his stomach.

George's act was next. At first he thought maybe it was just nervous butterflies in his tummy. But then the bubbling got **stronger**.

Oh no! Not the super burp! Not here in the middle of the circus.

George had to stop the bubbles. They **boing-bing-boinged** up to his chest.

They **bing-boing-binged** their way up his throat. And then . . .

George let out the loudest burp anyone had ever heard. It was louder than a tiger's roar! Louder than a wild boar's oink!

And then, George completely lost control. **The burp was in charge.**

George's feet raced over to the snack stand. His hands grabbed a soda bottle and began shaking it up and down. Then George burst into the ring.

"George! Go away!" Julianna shouted.

"Our act's not over."

George's ears didn't listen to Julianna. His fingers started untwisting the cap on the soda bottle . . . **BOOM**! The bubbly soda exploded out of the bottle—and sprayed all over the kids and the parents.

"Hey! What are you doing?" one of the dads shouted.

"George, cut it out!" Julianna ordered.

But the super burp wouldn't be tamed. George kept spraying the soda until the bottle was empty. Then he ran

back to the snack table, and grabbed the Boston cream pie.

"George, no!" Chris shouted out.

George wanted to put the pie down. But his hands wouldn't cooperate.

George's legs started running around the ring. "Get ready to see a **pie fly**!" he shouted out to the crowd.

"Pies can't fly," a little girl shouted back.

"Wanna bet?" George asked. He stopped running. He raised his eyebrows and grinned. Slowly, George drew back

one arm and took aim—right at Julianna.

"George! Don't you dare—," Julianna
began.

Too late! The ooey-gooey Boston cream
pie was already soaring through the air.

Julianna was quick. She ducked, and
the pie flew right over her head—and hit
Alex in the face!

The kids in the audience started to
laugh **really hard**.

"What was that for?" Alex shouted.
Chocolate goo and whipped cream was
dripping all over him.

George didn't answer.
Instead, he headed for the
small trampoline.

"Georgie!" Sage shouted. "No
fair! That's *my* act."

George scrambled onto the

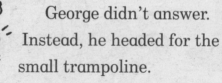

trampoline and began jumping.

Boing! Boing! Boing! George bounced **higher and higher** on the trampoline.

"Whee! I'm flying," he cried.

Boing! Boing! George wiggled his rear end for the crowd.

"Ha-ha-ha!" The kids were all laughing.

Boing! George bounced up again. But this time it felt like someone snatched him from behind.

George was hanging in midair. His arms waved. His legs kicked wildly.

The kids laughed harder.

George turned to see what had happened. *Oh no!* He was hanging from the branch of a tree—by **his *underwear***!

And then . . . suddenly . . . *whoosh!* George felt something pop deep in his belly. It felt like the wind had been knocked right out of him. **The super burp was gone.**

"Ow!" George cried out. "I'm stuck! Get me down from here."

"I'll get a ladder," Chris yelled.

Alex was still wiping goo off his face. "Mmmm . . . I guess the show is over," he told the crowd.

"A five-minute circus?" one dad said. "I want my **money back**."

"So do I," a mom said.

"I didn't even get to do my act," Sage complained.

"Stop groaning!" George said. "*I'm* the one with **the world's worst wedgie**."

Chris returned with the ladder. Julianna held it steady at the bottom as Chris climbed up. He pulled on the branch.

Crack. The branch **broke**. George landed on the ground—**hard**.

Chris looked at the broken tree branch. "My parents aren't going to be happy when they see this," Chris said.

George wasn't happy, either. He was pretty sure he had a splinter in his backside.

Stupid super burp. It had ruined everything . . . again.

Chapter 8

On Monday, the first thing Louie said to George was, "I heard about your circus. You really **cracked** people up."

George didn't say anything.

Max and Mike both said, "Good one, Louie."

"Why would you have a circus, anyway?" Louie said. "Circuses are for **babies**."

"Because we want to buy . . . ," Chris started.

George nudged him in the side before he could finish the sentence. He didn't want Louie to know they were saving up for a remote-controlled Dude-on-a-Skateboard. Louie would **never shut up** about getting one first.

"We like being in business," George said.

"So exactly how much have you made?" Louie asked him.

"Uh, the bell's about to ring," Alex said.

"Right behind you," George said.

"Behind . . ." Louie laughed **in a mean way**. "Good one, George."

* . •◗• ₚ
₀ • ◗ ₀ • .

"Mrs. Kelly, are you okay?" Sage asked.

Mrs. Kelly had red scratches on her arms, and a long scratch on her cheek.

"My sweet kitty cat, Fester, got upset," Mrs. Kelly said.

"It looks like she got attacked by a boar," Alex whispered to George. "And not the pink piggy kind of boar. **The wild kind.**"

The old George would have laughed at that. But George was still trying to be the new, improved George.

"It wasn't actually Fester's fault," Mrs. Kelly explained. "I was cat-sitting for a friend and Fester isn't used to having another kitty in the house. They got into a fight and I got caught in the middle. But I'd never let **my little kitty witty** get hurt."

George choked back another laugh.

"I love all kinds of cats. Fester's a Manx cat. But Siamese cats are beautiful, too," Mrs. Kelly said.

"My family went to Africa on a safari," Louie told Mrs. Kelly. "We saw tigers. Even **a white tiger**."

George rolled his eyes. Louie was always showing off.

"Are we going to study cats?" Sage asked.

"No," Mrs. Kelly told Sage. "We're just having a conversation about pets and the way people love them. After gym class, we'll go back to our unit on Alaska and the Arctic."

"We have gym first this morning?" Alex asked.

Mrs. Kelly nodded. "Except Mr. Trainer isn't here, so I'm your gym teacher today."

George frowned. How come Mr. Trainer was absent so much?

"In fact . . ." Mrs. Kelly's voice drifted off while **a huge, gummy smile** formed on her face.

George gulped. He knew that smile. It was the smile Mrs. Kelly got just before she made the class do something **awful**.

"Do you all know the alley cat dance?" Mrs. Kelly asked the class when they arrived at the gym.

"I don't," Louie said.

"Me neither," Julianna added.

"Well, I'll teach it to you right now," Mrs. Kelly said. "Just do what I do."

Mrs. Kelly took dancing **very seriously**. The only way you could get out of one of her dances would be if you had a broken leg. And then she might still make you dance—on your crutches.

Mrs. Kelly put her hands up in front, like cat paws. Then she started to dance. "Right foot. Right foot. Left foot. Left," she sang as she danced. "Right knee.

Right knee. Left knee. Left. And clap and turn."

George frowned. Then it hit him. Something Mrs. Kelly had said was really interesting. Not the right foot, left foot stuff. The thing about people really loving pets. A **big smile** formed on George's face. He knew the perfect business to go into. **This one couldn't miss.**

Chapter 9

"As soon as these hamsters start having babies, we'll make a fortune," George told Chris and Alex. It was Saturday. The boys were in the shed behind George's house.

"I don't know," Chris said. "So far all we've done is **lose** money."

"**Remember what Mrs. Kelly said** about people loving their pets?" George asked. "Who wouldn't love to bring home a cute baby hamster? And we'll have a big supply soon. Hamsters can have as many as seven babies at one time. I read that on a hamster website."

"Maybe that's why Mr. Furstman gave us such a good deal on these hamsters," Alex said.

"Mr. Furstman is a nice guy," George said. Mr. Furstman had also loaned

George a big hamster cage. "I know him because his pet shop is in the same shopping center as my mom's store."

"We have two boy hamsters and two girl hamsters," Chris said. "If the girls both have seven babies . . ."

"We'll have **fourteen new hamsters**," Alex said. "And if we sell them at two dollars a piece, we'll

have enough money to buy
the Dude, and earn back
everything we paid
for the food and
stuff."

"Is your
mom okay with us
keeping the hamsters
in here?" Chris asked.

Actually, George had **no idea** if his
mom was okay with it, mostly because
he hadn't asked her. He wasn't exactly
trying to hide the hamsters from his
mom. That was something the old George
would do. *This* George was trying to be
responsible. If the hamsters kept having
babies, before long, George would be able
to pay his mom back for
the ruined material and
broken beads at the

Knit Wit. Paying his mom back would show **maturity**. His mom loved stuff like that, **even more than his special face**.

Besides, George figured his parents wouldn't ever find out about the hamsters. Neither of them ever came into the shed. It was filled with boxes of things from their old house in Cherrydale.

"We have to make sure the cage is kept clean. And they need a lot of water," George told Alex and Chris. "And chew sticks. **Hamsters love chew sticks**."

"You know a lot about hamsters," Chris said.

"Our third-grade class pet at my old school was a hamster," George told him.

George picked

up one of the hamsters and pet it gently on the back. All four of its feet were white. It looked like it was wearing socks.

"At first I was creeped out by Speedy," George said. "Especially when he escaped and wound up in my sneaker. But I got to like him. In fact, this one kind of looks like Speedy. I'm naming it **Speedy 2**."

George stuck an extra chew stick into Speedy 2's cage. "Don't worry," he told the hamster. "I'll come back later and visit."

George did come back. In fact, over the next few days, George spent a lot of his free time in the shed behind his house. He loved being with the hamsters. And lucky for him, the super burp left him alone while he was there. When George was with the hamsters, there wasn't even one mini-bubble in his belly.

Alex and Chris helped out, too. One afternoon when George had to go to the dentist, Alex fed all the hamsters. The next morning, Chris came over and fed them before picking up George for school.

"Speedy 2 is getting **really fat**," Chris said as the boys walked toward school. "Do you think she's a girl hamster and she's going to have babies soon?"

George shrugged. "Maybe. Or it could be that I give her extra treats."

"You shouldn't have favorites, George," Chris said. "We have to like all the hamsters the same."

"I know," George agreed. But **he couldn't help himself**. Speedy 2 was his favorite. It would be kind of cool if she really was getting

ready to have babies. Then there would be **Speedys 3, 4, 5, 6, 7, 8, and 9!**

George ran home from school to see if Chris had been right about Speedy 2 being ready to be a mom.

When George got to the shed, there was a surprise waiting for him. **But it wasn't a hamster mom.** It was a human mom. *George's* mom.

"George, do you know why these **rats** are in my shed?" his mom asked angrily, pointing to the hamster cage.

"They're not rats,

Mom. They're hamsters," George told her.

"I don't care what they are," his mom said. "I want to know why they're here."

"They're going to have babies," he said. "And then Alex, Chris, and I are going to sell them. We're in the **hamster business**."

"You *were* in the hamster business," George's mom said. "Now you're out of it."

"Why?" George asked her.

"Because one of your pets escaped," his mother explained. "It chewed a hole in one of the boxes."

"Hamsters love to chew," George said.

"I figured that out," George's mother told him. "The hamster chewed a hole in a sweater I knitted this summer. His mom held up a blue sweater with a big hole in the front.

Oh man. **This was *ba-a-d*.** But the sweater hole wasn't the worst of it. When George turned to look at the cage, he realized something awful. The missing hamster was Speedy 2. Chris must not have closed her cage door all the way when he cleaned it that morning.

"Poor Speedy 2," George said. "I have to find her!"

"Yes, you do," his mom agreed.

George got a really worried look on his face. Speedy 2 was **so small**. She could have slipped out from under the door or through a hole in the shed. It was a big world out there. She could be lost . . . **or worse**.

"It's all my fault!" George said. "I can't do anything right."

George's mom took a deep breath. "Look, George, I'm really proud that you tried to start your own business. But animals are a big responsibility. And you should have asked permission."

"I know," George said. "I'm really sorry."

"Once you find the missing hamster," his mother said, "take them all back to the pet shop."

George looked under boxes and in between cartons. He looked on the top shelves. And on the bottom shelves. And then . . . *whish!* Something **small and furry** zoomed across the floor toward the corner of the shed.

George scooped Speedy 2 up in his hands. **Her little hamster heart was beating really fast.**

"Boy, am I going to miss you," he told the hamster.

Chapter 10

"Wow! Mr. Furstman gave us all our money back," Chris said.

"So how come you look so bummed?" Alex asked. "Is it about the RC Dude-on-a-Skateboard?"

"Nah," he said. **"I miss Speedy 2."**

"Can you visit her?" Chris asked him.

"Yeah," George said. "Mr. Furstman said I can stop by the pet shop any time."

"Let's go after school," Chris suggested. "I have to go to the stationery store across the street to get a new blank book. I'm starting another comic book. It's called *Toiletman: Escape from Under the Lid.*"

"Aroo! Ruff! Ruff!"

"Tweet! Tweet!"

"Meow!"

Things were really crazy in Mr. Furstman's pet shop when George got there. Poor Mr. Furstman could **barely keep up**. At the moment, he was busy trying to catch a goldfish and put it in a bag of water for a little girl.

"I want the one that's really **golden**," George heard the little girl tell her mother and Mr. Furstman.

All goldfish looked the same to George. But not to the little girl. When Mr. Furstman handed her a bag with a goldfish in it, she started to yell.

"No!" she shouted. "Not him. **I want the golden one**!"

Just then, a man with a small, brown, furry dog walked up behind Mr. Furstman. "Where do you keep the Pupper Supper dog food?" he asked him. "That's the kind Bruiser likes."

"Third aisle, on the left," Mr. Furstman told him.

"I looked there. I didn't see it," the man said.

George looked over at Mr. Furstman. **He seemed really frazzled.**

"Can I help?" George said.

Mr. Furstman looked up from the fish tank and shot George a smile. "Thanks, George," he said.

"No problem," George answered.

George found the dog food for the man and then went to the next aisle, where the hamster cages were. He was looking for Speedy 2 when Mr. Furstman called out, "George, can you show this woman where the chew sticks are?"

"Sure." George waved to the woman. "They're right over here."

When things calmed down, George went back to check on Speedy 2. Mr. Furstman came over.

"I think she's going to have a litter of babies very soon," Mr. Furstman said.

"Wow," George said. "You're so **lucky**, Mr. Furstman. You get to be around animals all the time."

"It's a good job," Mr. Furstman said. "I love animals. And I like people who love animals, too. You were a big help today. Maybe you'd like to help out more often."

"You mean like **a job**?" George asked.

Mr. Furstman nodded. "You could earn a little extra money and . . ."

"Visit Speedy 2!" George finished Mr. Furstman's sentence.

"Exactly," Mr. Furstman said.

Wow. This was perfect. Or at least
it would be as long as the stupid super
burp stayed away.

Chapter 11

"Say hi, Petey. Hi," George told the green parrot who sat in a cage in the middle of the pet store. "Hi."

"Squawk!" Petey answered.

George rolled his eyes. He'd been trying for three weeks to get Petey to say "hi." But all he did was squawk.

Still, George wasn't giving up. Petey was his best friend in the whole pet store. Speedy 2 had already had her babies, and she was back in a cage with other hamsters. One of her babies had white socks, too.

But Petey was the only parrot in the pet shop, and **he loved George**—especially when George let him ride around on his shoulder. George liked that, too. It made him feel like a **pirate**.

"Say hi," George told Petey again.

"Squawk," Petey answered.

Just then, bells began to ring. That meant someone was coming in. George looked up. It was Alex and Chris.

"Yo, dudes!" George shouted out.

"We came to visit the hamsters," Chris said.

"George, can you feed the garter snakes?" Mr. Furstman called.

"Sure thing, Mr. Furstman." George turned to his friends. "I gotta work."

"Can we watch you feed the snakes?" Alex asked.

"Sure," George said. "But I'm warning you—**it's not pretty**."

George walked over to where Mr. Furstman kept the snake food. Some kids might be freaked out by having to stick their hands into a vat of **wiggly, jiggly** worms.

But not George. Worms were what garter snakes ate.

"Yuck," Chris said. "Aren't they slimy?"

"*Super* slimy," George said. "And they smell, too."

"Wow," Alex said. **"That's so cool."**

George proudly carried a handful of wiggly, jiggly, slimy worms over to the snake cages. **"Dinner time!"** he called out.

Just then a woman carrying a little, white dog walked up behind George. "Young man," she asked. "Do you sell **gourmet** dog food?"

George turned around. The dog was wearing a jeweled collar. The woman was wearing a jeweled necklace. They matched—in a weird **dog, dog-owner** kind of way.

"We sell dog food," George said. "I don't know if it's gourmet."

George was about to say he'd ask

Mr. Furstman, when suddenly something bubbly began wiggling around in his belly. Kind of like a worm.

George hadn't burped once during the three weeks he'd been working at the pet shop. And he wasn't about to let it happen now. He shut his lips tight.

But the burp was **strong**. It had already bounced its way out of his belly and into his chest. Now it was heading straight for his mouth.

"Burp . . ." A tiny little burp slipped out from between George's clenched lips. It wasn't a **supersonic mega burp**, but it was a magic burp. And now it was out there.

"Young man!" the woman scolded. "That's disgusting. You should say '**excuse me**.'"

George knew that was true. But he also knew he couldn't say that—or anything else. He was afraid to open his mouth. A bigger burp might slip out.

"Now where is the dog food?" the woman said.

George reached out his hand and pointed to the dog food aisle.

"Aaah!" the rich woman shouted. She almost dropped her dog.

George looked at his hand. *Uh-oh.* He'd just pointed to the dog food with some worms dangling from his fingers.

"Get those things out of my sight!" the woman told George.

That was all it took. **The burp could no longer be controlled.** It just had to do something funny. George's mouth popped open. And his hand dropped the worms right down his throat.

The worms wiggled inside his mouth. *Gulp.* George's throat swallowed hard. Down went the wiggling, jiggling worms **right into George's belly**.

The woman looked like she was going to faint.

"Whoa!" Chris shouted. "Dude! I can't believe you did that!"

"Awesome!" Alex added. He sounded seriously impressed.

Whoosh. Just then George felt something go pop deep inside. Sort of like a needle bursting a balloon. It was like the air went rushing out of him.

Unfortunately, the customer rushed out, too. "I'll never come back here again," she said in a loud voice—loud enough for Mr. Furstman to hear.

"George!" Mr. Furstman shouted as he ran across the store.

Uh-oh. Was George about to lose another job?

"You guys better get out of here," George told Alex and Chris. "Go look at the hamsters or something."

Alex and Chris nodded. They hurried away before Mr. Furstman got to where George was standing.

"Are you okay?" Mr. Furstman asked George.

Huh? George was pretty confused. **He was fine.**

"That dog bit me once," Mr. Furstman told him. "So when I see him, I get nervous."

George shook his head. "Nah. He didn't bite me. But his owner said she wasn't ever coming back here."

"That's fine with me," Mr. Furstman told George. "She never buys anything, anyway. She just complains that we don't sell anything fancy enough for her **precious pooch**."

George laughed. The way Mr. Furstman had said "precious pooch" sounded just like the lady.

"You okay to go restock the kitty litter shelves?" Mr. Furstman asked George.

"Sure thing!" George said happily.

As he walked off to get the kitty litter, George smiled. He still had a job.

Take that, super burp!

Chapter 12

"Hi, Mr. Tyler," George said as he, Alex, Chris, and Julianna walked into the toy store on Sunday morning. "We're here to buy the remote-controlled Dude-on-a-Skateboard."

"I still can't believe we **really have all the money we need**," Alex whispered excitedly.

George nodded. "And a couple of dollars left over for extra batteries."

"Awesome!" Chris and Julianna said.

Mr. Tyler looked at the kids and shook his head. **"I'm sorry,"** he said, "but I sold the last one yesterday."

"No way," Alex said.

"You gotta be kidding," Chris added.

George didn't say anything. He couldn't. He was too bummed to talk.

"But I have some other cool toys," Mr. Tyler said. "How about a really amazing **chemistry set**?"

George shook his head. "I don't think my parents would want me to get anything where I could blow up stuff."

"Me neither," Chris agreed.

"The only thing we really wanted was the Dude-on-a-Skateboard," Julianna said.

"I'm sorry," Mr. Tyler said. "I guess you should have come in sooner."

"We didn't have the money sooner," Alex said.

George looked at the floor. He **knew it was his fault** they hadn't gotten the money in time. Well, not his fault, really. **The super burp's fault.**

George and his pals were not in very good moods when they left the toy store. As they passed by the park, they spotted Louie, Max, and Mike. Louie was kicking and stomping something on the ground.

"I wonder what that's all about," Julianna said.

"Let's go see," George said. He and his friends turned and walked into the park.

"Hey, Louie, what's up?" George asked.

"He's **mad**," Mike said.

"*Real* mad," Max added.

"At what?" George asked.

"At this stupid Dude-on-a-Skateboard," Louie grumbled. "What a hunk of junk."

"It's junk," Max agreed.

"A whole hunk," Mike added.

"What happened to it?" Alex asked.

"It popped a wheel," Louie said.

"You mean **it popped a *wheelie***," George corrected him.

Louie shook his head. "No. I mean it popped a wheel. The back wheel fell off. And then the dude's arm broke in half. **Stupid toy**!"

"Wow, that's too bad," George said.

"It's gonna be too bad for that toy store!" Louis shouted. "If they don't give me my money back, my dad's gonna sue them. **He's a big-time lawyer, you know.**"

George *didn't* know that. And he had never heard of anyone suing a toy store over a fifteen dollar toy, either. But he *was* glad he'd found out **the Dude-on-a-Skateboard toy wasn't so great**, after all.

He turned to his friends. "We gotta get going, right, guys?"

Julianna, Alex, and Chris nodded.

As they walked away, Alex said, "Boy, that was close."

"I know," Chris said.

"I can't believe we almost wasted fifteen dollars on a remote-controlled **hunk of junk**," George said.

"I guess we were lucky it took us so long to get the money," Julianna said.

George smiled. He knew luck had

nothing to do with it. The super burp
was what had kept them from getting the
money fast enough.

Amazing. George was **actually glad**
about something the super burp had
done. But just this once.

About the Author

Nancy Krulik is the author of more than 150 books for children and young adults including three *New York Times* best sellers and the popular Katie Kazoo, Switcheroo books. She lives in New York City with her family, and many of George Brown's escapades are based on things her own kids have done. (No one delivers a good burp quite like Nancy's son, Ian!) Nancy's favorite thing to do is laugh, which comes in pretty handy when you're trying to write funny books!

About the Illustrator

Aaron Blecha was raised by a school of giant squid in Wisconsin and now lives with his wife in London, England. He works as an artist and animator designing toys, making cartoons, and illustrating books, including the Zombiekins series. You can enjoy more of his weird creations at www.monstersquid.com.